The Adventures of KITTY BABY

STORY and ILLUSTRATION by FRED BEEMAN

The Adventures of Kitty Baby

Story and Illustration by Fred Beeman
Edited by Joanna Fee

Pizza Party In The Woodz
5212 Highland View Avenue
Los Angeles CA 90041

Email: pizzapartyinthewoods@gmail.com
ISBN 979-8-88862-879-9

Printed In the United States of America

In memory of one of the most fantastic,
little creatures I've ever known.

A cold wind blew through northern California.

A little cat named Kitty Baby waited patiently for his friend to come home.

SWOOOO

The wind swirled all around.

HOOT
HOOT

A large owl flew through the starry night sky, then landed on top of a nearby pine tree.

Kitty Baby sat shivering,

and alone,

remembering the last time he felt like this...

Sometime before…

Kitty Baby was scared, cold, and hungry one brisk January morning.

A young man named Charlie saw Kitty Baby and put down a pile of cat food hoping to help the little cat.

Kitty Baby waited for Charlie to leave before venturing out. His sheer size was enough to scare him straight out of his fur!

Once he knew he was safe, the golden little kitty trotted up to the kibble and began to eat.

CRUNCH
CRUNCH
CRUNCH

It had been a long time since Kitty Baby had a good meal.

Kitty Baby paused and looked up.

He saw another pile of dry cat food.

The little cat looked left and looked right,

then trotted up to the next pile of food.

It all tasted so good! For a little while, Kitty Baby felt safe and happy.

A couple of days went by. Kitty Baby was slowly becoming more trusting of Charlie.

One night, Kitty Baby felt safe enough to eat the food right off the old house steps.

Charlie watched Kitty Baby and smiled. He was sitting on his favorite chair, drinking his favorite soda, and watching cartoons.

Kitty Baby decided to peak his head inside the house. There he saw one last pile of treats on a clean plate.

The little golden cat proceeded to eat the last pile of dry cat food Charlie had left out for him.

Once he had a belly full of food, Kitty Baby sat across the room and smiled at his new friend.

Suddenly, Charlie's roommates arrived back at the old house. They were all talking very loudly while making a lot of noise! This scared Kitty Baby.

He jumped up and scrammed. That made Charlie sad, but he hoped to see Kitty Baby again soon.

A few days later,

Charlie came home from a long day of work.

He turned off the car's engine, and slowly got out of his vehicle.

He headed into the house carrying a couple of bags of groceries.

Charlie walked through the front door and into the kitchen.

He saw his roommate talking away on his cell phone.

Outside in the bushes, Kitty Baby had been waiting for Charlie. It felt like he was waiting forever.

When he saw the light turn on inside Charlie's room he was so excited!

The back door flew open. The young man put down the plate of food for his little feline friend.

Kitty Baby joyfully ran through the tall grass and up to the porch to say hi to Charlie.

Kitty Baby nudged up against Charlie's legs.

Charlie petted Kitty Baby's little golden head.

Then he got a bowl of fresh drinking water for Kitty Baby.

They were both very happy as they sat outside enjoying the night together.

As time went on, Kitty Baby and Charlie started spending more time together outside.

One night, Kitty Baby and Charlie walked through a vast orchard of fruit trees.

A large crescent moon hovered above the nearby mountain tops. Scattered purple clouds moved across the starry night sky.

Kitty Baby decided to stop and sharpen his unusually large claws on a nearby tree trunk.

Kitty Baby thought about how fun it would be to climb the tree.

Kitty Baby felt brave. He started climbing up the tree, holding on tight with his freshly sharpened claws.

Once he reached the top, he perched himself on the highest branch. He looked out over the sky full of stars.

Kitty Baby looked down toward his friend.

Charlie was smiling from ear to ear!

He was amazed by the golden feline.

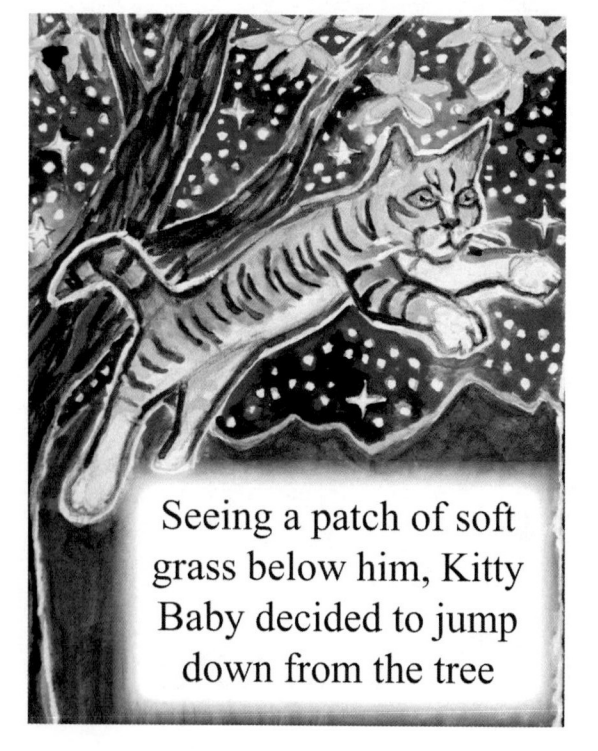

Seeing a patch of soft grass below him, Kitty Baby decided to jump down from the tree

and took flight into the air, just like a flying squirrel.

Kitty Baby's daydream
ended as he returned
from his fun memories
with Charlie.

He continued to
huddle in the bushes.
Waiting for Charlie
to return home.

But Charlie never did.

Night turned into morning.

Kitty Baby was hungry!

Kitty Baby began walking down the road.

He came across a diner on the corner.

The back door burst open as a busy cook came out of the kitchen.

He tossed a garbage bag into a dumpster nearby. Kitty Baby could smell food.

There must be food in the garbage bag!

Kitty Baby waited until the cook walked away, then leapt on top of the dumpster and peeked down inside.

Jumping down onto the trash bags, he sniffed around for something to eat.

What Kitty Baby couldn't see was a garbage truck driving toward the diner!

Kitty Baby found some delicious Chinese food to feast.

The big green garbage truck
then roared around a corner,

heading straight
towards the dumpster.

Kitty Baby had finished up
some treats. For a moment
he was happy again.

Finally Kitty Baby heard the noise. Then he could feel the truck grab the dumpster and lift it into the air!

The garbage truck began lifting the dumpster that he was still inside of.

Kitty Baby panicked. What could he do now?

Kitty Baby felt the dumpster tilting.

It tilted until everything started to spill out!

Kitty Baby fell into the big green garbage truck.

Trash bags rained down after him and it was making his golden fur very dirty.

The garbage truck returned the empty dumpster to where it sat before.

And then quickly drove off down the street.

Inside the garbage truck, Kitty Baby was pinned under several heavy bags of trash.

The noisy green garbage truck sputtered down the block, shaking Kitty Baby around.

Kitty Baby cried, thinking he had been eaten by a monster!

The garbage truck went down a dusty dirt road,

leading to the city dump.

Kitty Baby was scared and confused. How would hc get out of this mess?

The big green truck entered the dump site, stopped, and began to unload all its trash.

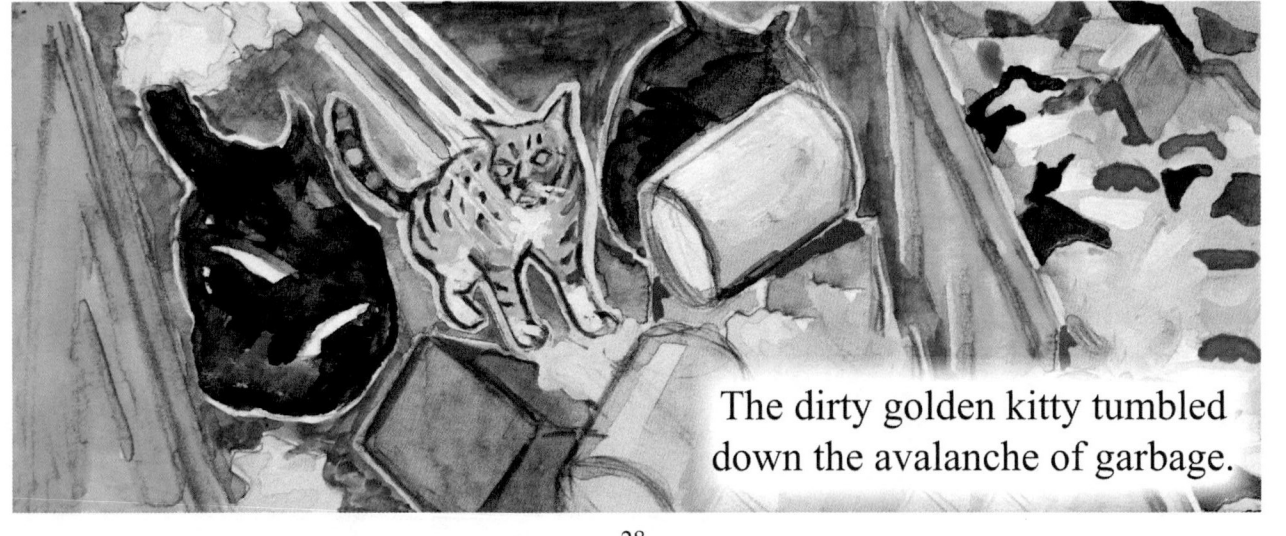

The dirty golden kitty tumbled down the avalanche of garbage.

Kitty Baby suddenly found himself free falling towards the ground.

He was able to land on his paws,

then leapt away from a tidal wave of filth.

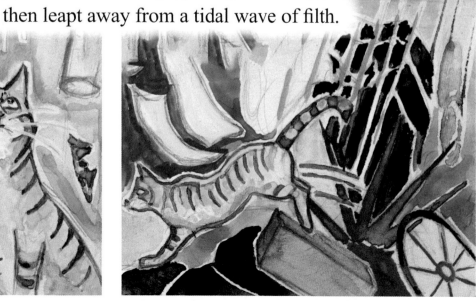

The large green garbage truck finished unloading and then drove off and out of sight.

Kitty Baby slowly began to make his way through the endless field of smelly trash.

He swiveled his little head from side to side, watching out for any signs of predators.

Kitty Baby was very tired as he walked through the dump graveyard, which seemed to go on forever.

Then something caught his eye—a couple of stray cats.

Thinking they might be friendly, Kitty Baby happily trotted up to the feline duo.

But friendly they were not. The two stray cats immediately hissed and growled at the little cat.

A large cat fight broke out.

Kitty Baby was back in survival mode. He swiped his large paws across the black cat's face. Meanwhile, the angry calico cat jumped up onto Kitty Baby's back.

Now the stunned black cat was mad!

Kitty Baby and the calico cat rolled around on the filthy ground.

Fur flew everywhere as Kitty Baby tried to fight off the meanest cats in the dump!

Just then, animal control showed up in a large, white city truck.

The noisy city truck chased after the three cats.

The truck cornered the injured black cat. An angry-looking woman holding a leash pole jumped out of the driver's seat and moved towards the cat.

As she got closer, the black cat hissed!

MEOW MEOW MEOW

The woman trapped the
black cat with a snare pole.

Then she put him
into a small cage.

This gave Kitty Baby and the other cat
a chance to run as fast as they could
towards a nearby chain-link fence.
It was their last hurdle to freedom!

Kitty Baby never looked back as he leapt high up into the air and latched himself onto the chain-link fence.

This time she was driving as fast as she could in pursuit of the last two feral cats.

The lady from animal control was back on the move.

The little golden cat climbed up the chain-link fence as quickly as he could. And the calico cat tried to follow Kitty Baby.

But as soon as he took flight, the calico kitty was caught by animal control.

Kitty Baby reached the other side and ran about as fast as his furry legs would carry him.

He bolted through an open field, and then up and over a hillside.

In the distance, Kitty Baby saw a train leaving its station. He knew what he had to do!

Seeing an open box car, Kitty Baby sprinted towards the train.

Kitty Baby leapt very high into the air. He had to use every ounce of energy he could muster.

He landed softly inside the train car. He could feel it start to move faster and faster.

Because of what happened at the dump, Kitty Baby didn't want to be seen by anyone! So he found a wooden crate and curled up inside.

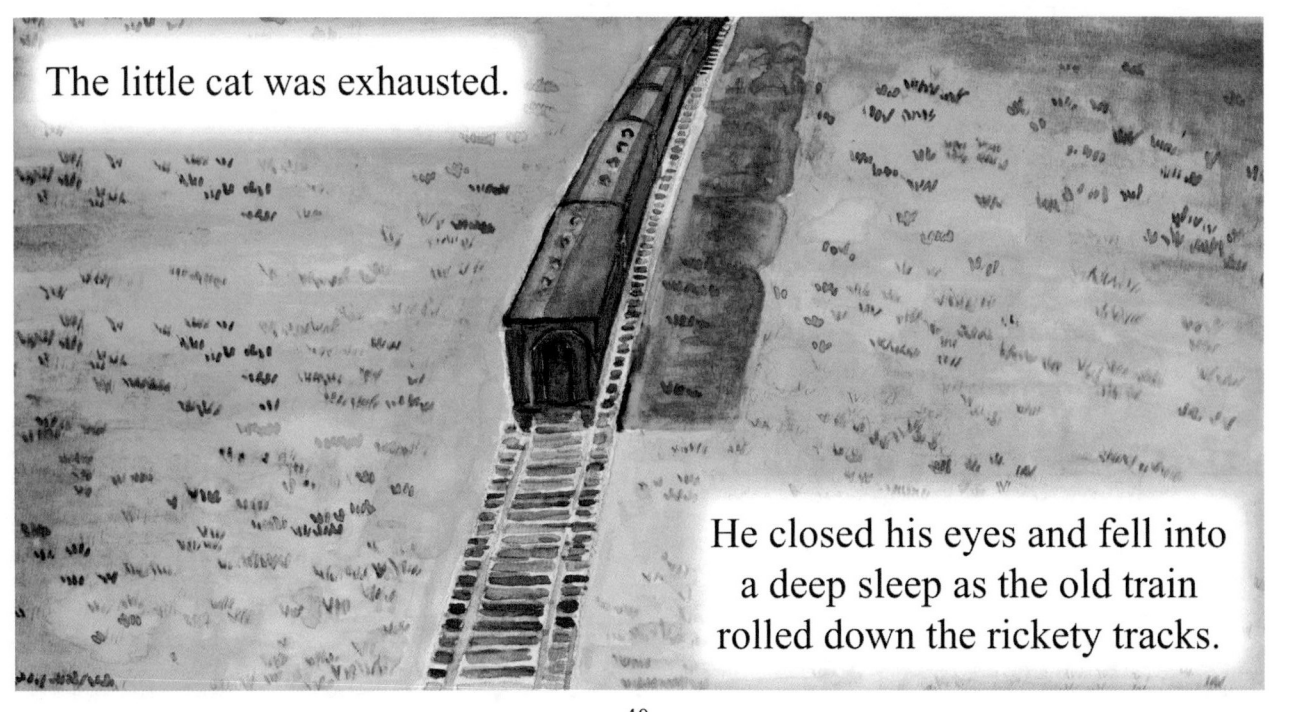

The little cat was exhausted.

He closed his eyes and fell into a deep sleep as the old train rolled down the rickety tracks.

Kitty Baby slept for a long time. He woke up suddenly to the feeling of a hard thud. The crate must have been loaded off the train.

He carefully peeked his little head from the shipping crate.

He saw it was safe to go out. Kitty Baby ran through a vast cargo hold filled with crates and boxes from the train.

Before him was an infinite blue sea. Kitty Baby gazed out at the vast Pacific Ocean.

Just then he was startled by the tremendous sound of a very loud foghorn.

At last, he came upon a narrow, worn-down stairwell.

Made in the USA
Las Vegas, NV
19 November 2022

59809093R00031